I0821399

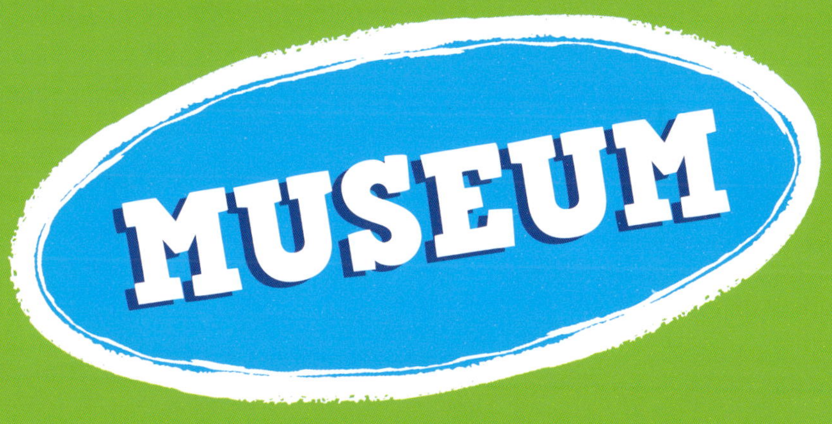

BY K.C. KELLEY

AMICUS READERS ● AMICUS INK

Amicus Readers and Amicus Ink are imprints of Amicus
P.O. Box 1329, Mankato, MN 56002
www.amicuspublishing.us

Cataloging-in-Publication Data is on file with the Library of Congress.
ISBN 978-1-68151-303-4 (library binding)
ISBN 978-1-68152-259-3 (paperback)
ISBN 978-1-68151-339-3 (eBook)

Editor: Sara Frederick
Designer: Patty Kelley
Photo Researcher/Producer: Shoreline Publishing Group LLC

Photo Credits:
Cover: Stock Foundry Images/Alamy Stock Photo
Alamy Stock: Lourens Smak 10; Dreamstime.com: Susan Sheldon 7, Marcio Silva 16T, Veikko Rihu 16R, Sunsear7 16L; Shutterstock: cowardlion 3, Uliya Krakos 5, Monkey Business Images 8, 12, Romrodphoto 15.

Printed in China.

HC 10 9 8 7 6 5 4 3 2 1
PB 10 9 8 7 6 5 4 3 2 1

Museums have wonderful things.
Let's explore a museum!

This is a science museum. Adam looks through a telescope.

How does gas
fill a bubble?
Brady finds out.

We learn about art.
Ann sees pottery
made long ago.
It is beautiful!

This dinosaur head is huge. It is much bigger than Ava. Look at those teeth!

Museum guides
help us.
Mr. Smith tells us
about fossils.

There is so much to see. Can we come back soon?

THINGS TO SEE AT A MUSEUM